Dear Parents and Educators,

Welcome to Penguin Young Readers! As parents and educators, you know that each child develops at his or her own pace—in terms of speech, critical thinking, and, of course, reading. Penguin Young Readers recognizes this fact. As a result, each Penguin Young Readers book is assigned a traditional easy-to-read level (1–4) as well as a Guided Reading Level (A–P). Both of these systems will help you choose the right book for your child. Please refer to the back of each book for specific leveling information. Penguin Young Readers features esteemed authors and illustrators, stories about favorite characters, fascinating nonfiction, and more!

Strawberry Shortcake™
School Friends

LEVEL 2

GUIDED
READING
LEVEL F

This book is perfect for a **Progressing Reader** who:
• can figure out unknown words by using picture and context clues;
• can recognize beginning, middle, and ending sounds;
• can make and confirm predictions about what will happen in the text; and
• can distinguish between fiction and nonfiction.

Here are some **activities** you can do during and after reading this book:
• Making Inferences: Making an inference means using what you know to make a guess about what you don't know, or reading between the lines. Reread pages 6–9. The author doesn't name the season, but can you make an inference and guess which season is coming? What clues did you use? Next, reread the text and look at the pictures on pages 14–15. How did the girls turn the bookstore into a classroom?
• Make Connections: Have you ever been scared to start school? Discuss how you overcame this fear.

Remember, sharing the love of reading with a child is the best gift you can give!

—Bonnie Bader, EdM
  Penguin Young Readers program

*Penguin Young Readers are leveled by independent reviewers applying the standards developed by Irene Fountas and Gay Su Pinnell in *Matching Books to Readers: Using Leveled Books in Guided Reading*, Heinemann, 1999.

Penguin Young Readers
Published by the Penguin Group
Penguin Group (USA) Inc., 375 Hudson Street, New York, New York 10014, USA
Penguin Group (Canada), 90 Eglinton Avenue East, Suite 700, Toronto, Ontario M4P 2Y3, Canada
(a division of Pearson Penguin Canada Inc.)
Penguin Books Ltd., 80 Strand, London WC2R 0RL, England
Penguin Group Ireland, 25 St. Stephen's Green, Dublin 2, Ireland (a division of Penguin Books Ltd.)
Penguin Group (Australia), 250 Camberwell Road, Camberwell, Victoria 3124, Australia
(a division of Pearson Australia Group Pty. Ltd.)
Penguin Books India Pvt. Ltd., 11 Community Centre, Panchsheel Park, New Delhi—110 017, India
Penguin Group (NZ), 67 Apollo Drive, Rosedale, Auckland 0632, New Zealand
(a division of Pearson New Zealand Ltd.)
Penguin Books (South Africa) (Pty.) Ltd., 24 Sturdee Avenue, Rosebank,
Johannesburg 2196, South Africa

Penguin Books Ltd., Registered Offices: 80 Strand, London WC2R 0RL, England

Strawberry Shortcake™ and related trademarks © 2012 Those Characters From Cleveland, Inc.
Used under license by Penguin Young Readers Group. Published by Penguin Young Readers,
an imprint of Penguin Group (USA) Inc., 345 Hudson Street, New York, New York 10014.
Manufactured in China.

ISBN 978-0-448-45877-9   10 9 8 7 6 5 4 3 2 1

 Strawberry Shortcake™

School Friends

by Lana Edelman

illustrated by MJ Illustrations

Penguin Young Readers

An Imprint of Penguin Group (USA) Inc.

It is nice outside.

Strawberry Shortcake plays

with her friends.

Look!

The leaves are red.

The leaves are orange.

The leaves are falling down.

Summer will be over soon.

It is almost time for school.

The Berrykins have never been
to school.

The Berrykins are scared.

Blueberry Muffin has

a great idea.

The girls can play school.

The Berrykins can

play the students.

Who will play the teacher?

The girls turn the bookstore

into a classroom.

The Berrykins are ready

to play the students.

One plus one is two.

Blueberry will teach reading.

The cat sat on a mat.

The cat
sat on
a mat.

Lemon Meringue will

teach science.

Mix! Mix! Mix!

Plum Pudding will teach gym.

Throw and catch!

Oh no!

Raspberry Torte is sad.

What will she teach

the Berrykins?

The girls want to help Raspberry.

Lemon has a great idea!

Raspberry can teach

the Berrykins about friendship.

Raspberry is a great friend.

Raspberry teaches the Berrykins
how to be good friends.

Raspberry is happy now.

The girls are finished
with their lessons.
The Berrykins are
ready for school!